Emma Jane's Aeroplane

For Angus. Let the adventure continue!
K.H.

For Florence
D.R.

A TEMPLAR BOOK

First published in the UK in 2017 by Templar Publishing,
part of the Bonnier Publishing Group,
The Plaza, 535 King's Road, London, SW10 0SZ
www.templarco.co.uk
www.bonnierpublishing.com

Illustration copyright © 2017 by Daniel Rieley
Design copyright © 2017 by Templar Publishing

1 3 5 7 9 10 8 6 4 2

ISBN 978-1-78370-840-6

Written by Katie Haworth
Edited by Ruth Symons
Designed by Olivia Cook

Printed in Lithuania

Emma Jane's Aeroplane

Written by
Katie Haworth

Illustrated by
Daniel Rieley

templar publishing

One bright night, Emma Jane
sets off in her aeroplane;
over lakes and over hills,
through the darkness calm and still.

Up ahead is something bright –
it's a city's shining lights . . .

It's London!

Round Big Ben she dips and loops,
high above the Thames she swoops.

And riding in the London Eye,
she finds a fox, who wants to fly.

So Emma Jane in her aeroplane,
and a fox who doesn't like the rain
fly on.

Up ahead is something bright –
it's a city's shining lights . . .

It's Paris!

Around the Eiffel Tower she spins,
she loops-the-loop and flips and skims.

On Notre Dame a rooster crows
and into the little plane he goes.

So Emma Jane in her aeroplane,
a fox who doesn't like the rain,
and a rooster who crows wherever he goes
fly on.

Up ahead is something bright –
it's a city's shining lights . . .

It's Venice!

The Grand Canal is wide and deep,
the gondoliers are fast asleep.

The St Mark's lion shakes his mane
and roars until he's on the plane!

So Emma Jane in her aeroplane,
a fox who doesn't like the rain,
a rooster who crows wherever he goes,
and a lion so proud he holds up his nose
fly on.

Up ahead is something bright –
it's a city's shining lights . . .

It's New York!

The Statue of Liberty's tall and strong,
and all Manhattan's lights are on.

Down on Broadway a pigeon's dance
leads to the plane with a hop and prance.

So Emma Jane in her aeroplane,
a fox who doesn't like the rain,
a rooster who crows wherever he goes,
a lion so proud he holds up his nose,
and a pigeon who sings and claps her wings
fly on.

Up ahead is something bright –
it's a city's shining lights . . .

It's Beijing!

On the Great Wall a dragon sings,
she wants the plane to give her wings!

The World Trade Centre sparkles bright,
the palace glows with twinkling lights.

So Emma Jane in her aeroplane,
a fox who doesn't like the rain,
a rooster who crows wherever he goes,
a lion so proud he holds up his nose,
a pigeon who sings and claps her wings,
and a dragon who wriggles and jiggles and giggles
fly on.

Up ahead is something bright –
it's a city's shining lights . . .

It's Sydney!

From the Harbour Bridge they admire the view,
the Opera House, and fireworks, too.

And from his surfboard on the tide
a wombat wants to hitch a ride.

So Emma Jane in her aeroplane,
a fox who doesn't like the rain,
a rooster who crows wherever he goes,
a lion so proud he holds up his nose,
a pigeon who sings and claps her wings,
a dragon who wriggles and jiggles and giggles,
and a wombat dude who's a little bit rude
fly on.

Up ahead, something's not right –
a darkening cloud, a flash of light . . .

On they fly through the stormy sky,
the rain beats down, the waves lash high,
and the plane is tossed by a fearsome wind
then into the churning sea it spins.

Whoosh!

Whirr!

Splash!

Now Emma Jane and her aeroplane
and her friends who came along,
are lost at sea on the ocean waves
and the night seems very long.

But the pigeon is good with directions
and she even brought a map.

The dragon mends the propellers
while the wombat bails with his hat.

The rooster has a foghorn crow,
the lion makes a sail.

While Emma Jane steers through the waves,
the fox rows with his tail.

And when they get back to the shore
they hug each other tight.

Then Emma Jane and all her friends
fly back in the dawn's pink light.

The wombat stays in Sydney,

and the dragon in Beijing.

ONE WAY

The pigeon goes back to New York
while dancing on the wing.

The lion steps off in St Mark's
and turns back into stone.

The rooster stays in Paris,
which is where he feels at home.

And Emma Jane farewells the fox
with morning in the sky.

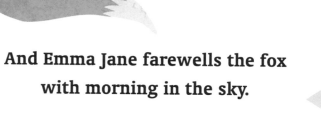

Then she zooms off in her plane . . .

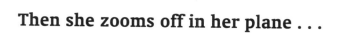

. . . where do you think she'll fly?

More picture books from Templar:

ISBN: 978-1-78370-418-7 (hardback)
978-1-78370-419-4 (paperback)

ISBN: 978-1-78370-389-0 (hardback)

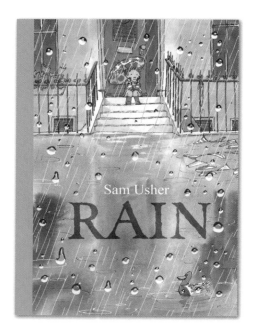

ISBN: 978-1-78370-546-7 (hardback)
978-1-78370-547-4 (paperback)

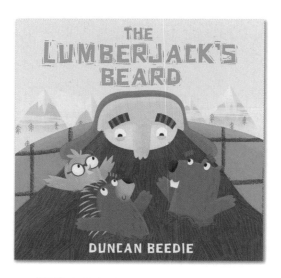

ISBN: 978-1-78370-687-7 (hardback)
978-1-78370-688-4 (paperback)

www.templarco.co.uk